Also by Jane Butel

FAVORITE MEXICAN FOODS

Food and Appliance Brochures for:

Con Edison
Edison Electric Institute
General Electric
Heublein
Hotpoint
Public Service Company of New Mexico